Daniel Finds His Voice

By Sheletta Brundidge
and Lily Coyle

Pictures by
Darcy Bell-Myers

To my great grandmother, Mrs. Mary Freddie Welcome,
for praying and pushing me into my purpose; and to all the music
teachers and music therapists working with kids who have autism,
I see you and applaud you. — S.B.

To Weird Al, you make it look so easy. — L.C.

For Rhys, who has found his true voice — D.B.M.

Very Special Thanks

TO LIL NAS X

*for creating our favorite song
and for helping Daniel find his voice*

Illustrated by Darcy Bell-Myers
ISBN: 978-1-64343-801-6 hardcover
       978-1-64343-698-2 softcover
Library of Congress Control Number: 2021902109
Printed in The United States
First Printing: 2021

Cover and interior design by Darcy Bell-Myers
Written by Sheletta Brundidge and Lily Coyle

"Daniel Finds His Voice" First softcover edition 2022
Copyright 2021 by Sheletta Brundidge

The original publication of this book was printed in bulk using a traditional offset printing process. This copy, however, was printed "on demand" using different materials and printing processes, and while it may vary in several ways from the original, the content is the same. Printing on demand makes it possible for this independent author's book to stay in print long after the original publication date and leaves a much smaller environmental footprint. Thank you for supporting this independently published book!

Beaver's Pond Press, Inc.
939 Seventh Street West
St. Paul, MN 55102
(952) 829-8818
www.BeaversPondPress.com

To order, visit www.ItascaBooks.com
Reseller discounts available.

Darcy Bell-Myers
Illustration & Design
www.bellmyers.com

SHElettaMakesMeLaugh.com

I'm Daniel, the youngest Brundidge Baby.
My mom won an RV in a contest.

Now we can visit Grandma Mary.
She is about to turn a hundred
years old and she lives in an old
town very far away.

Dad takes our RV on the big city freeway.

I sing my favorite song.
I have autism and I like to sing better than I like to talk.

Gonna ride 'til I can't no more . . .

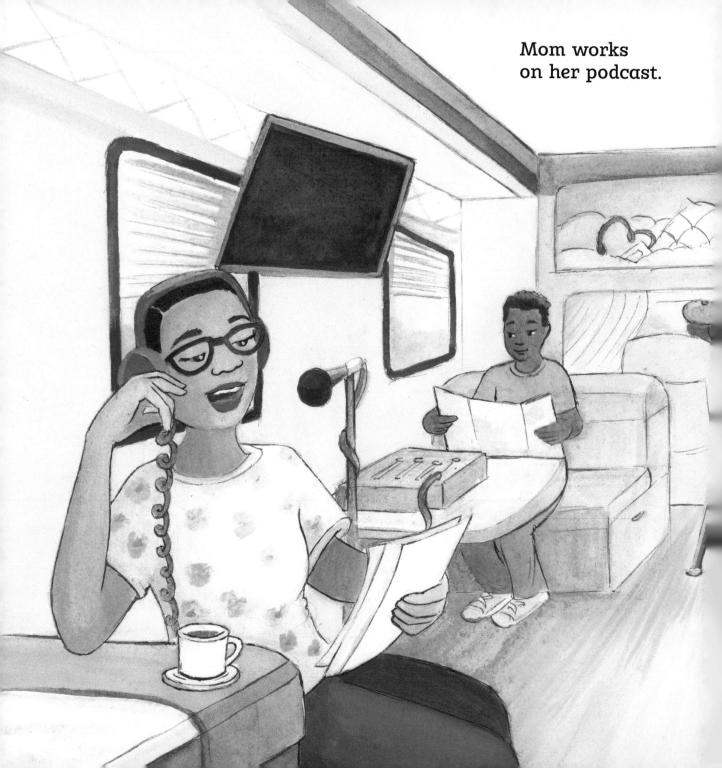

Mom works
on her podcast.

Brandon counts cars and trucks and keeps track of their colors.

He has autism too. Counting is something he likes to do.

Dad drives
'til he can't no more.
Then we stop for gas.

Dad cooks his special spaghetti.

Cameron reads her books. She has autism too. Reading is something she likes to do.

Andrew can't drive. He doesn't have his permit yet. So he just studies the map. Andrew does not have autism. But he is a teenager.

I sing my favorite song.

Gonna ride
'til I can't no more . . .

Mom drives 'til she can't no more. Then we stop to sleep.

We wake up extra early like we always do.

Dad takes our RV on the old town road. I shout,

THEY CAN'T RIDE NO MORE!

Hundred Years Old

Yeah, we're gonna see our grandma turn a hundred years old
We're gonna ride 'til we can't no more
We're gonna see our grandma turn a hundred years old
We're gonna ride 'til we can't no more

Cameron reading in the back
Andrew looking at the map
Dad is cooking food from scratch
Mom lays down a podcast track

Daniel sees a horse, ha
Brandon counting Porsche
Gassed up in the valley
Our grandma's waiting on that porch, now

Sing a song to tell you something
Sing to tell you something
Sing a song to tell you something
Sing to tell you something

Passing by a tractor
Airplane would be faster
But we love our RV
All Mom's prayers were answered

Music coming through me
Melody speaks to me
Lyrics bring it to me
Singing is the true me

Sing a song to tell you something
Sing to tell you something
Sing a song to tell you something
Sing to tell you something

Yeah, we're gonna see our grandma turn a hundred years old
We're gonna ride 'til we can't no more
We're gonna see our grandma turn a hundred years old
We're gonna ride 'til we can't no more

A Few Good Things to Know about Autism and Music

Many people love music, for many different reasons. If you have autism, music might play a special role in your life.

No two people with autism are the same. One might be the best trumpet player in the world, while another might hate trumpets!

Music reaches our brains in ways that words can't. Teachers and therapists often use music to help people learn, grow, or heal. Music can improve behavior, speech, focus, communication, relationships, stress, and anxiety. This is true whether you have autism or not.

Music might be the "language" you use to communicate, if you have autism. You might express yourself better by singing than by speaking. This is also true of some people who stutter or have speech issues, and of some people who just really like to sing and write songs!

The rhythm and repeating patterns in music might give you an extra strong feeling of calm or joy if you have autism. You might like playing or hearing one song over and over, again and again.

You might have a special talent for reading, practicing, memorizing, or playing music if you have autism. Or you might know a lot of facts about a certain artist or type of music.

If you have autism—or not—you might find it easier to make friends by sharing the music you love. Music brings people together, and sometimes it helps people feel a sense of belonging. If you want to make new friends, try sharing your favorite music with them and asking about theirs!